Meet the New Boss

Meet the New Boss

Tom Black

SEA LION PRESS

First published by Sea Lion Press, 2015
Copyright © 2015 Tom Black
All rights reserved.
ISBN: 9798370687280
Cover artwork by Jack Tindale

This book is a work of fiction. While 'real-world' characters may appear, the nature of the divergent story means any depictions herein are fictionalised and in no way an indication of real events. Above all, characterisations have been developed with the primary aim of telling a compelling story.

"Meet the new boss, same as the old boss."

The Who - Won't Get Fooled Again

1940-1946 David Lloyd George

National Action Party

The Man Who Won The War – and lost the next one

The actions taken by David Lloyd George in 1940 divide scholarly opinion worldwide even to this day. At the time, as German shells fell on London's East End and Churchill lay dead in a destroyed railway carriage, it seemed to the grand old man of British politics that there was no other option. Of course, there was - to fight, fight and fight again. To never surrender to fascism. But this choice was, tragically, not acceptable to the man who, incredibly, was at the time Britain's greatest living statesman.

However, even Lloyd George's harshest critics accept that his actions - the visit to the King, formation of a government and immediate armistice negotiation were all motivated by a determination to spare Britain another destructive war. 'The Man Who Won The War' was committed to ending this one. But, in doing so, the Welsh Wizard became the Welsh Weasel.

The formation of the National Action Party in December 1940 saw Lloyd George, Harold Nicolson, J.F.C. Fuller and others form a cabinet, with Lloyd George moving into Number 10. The legacy of his predecessors was there for him to behold. The Plymouth Room still bore the garish, huge photograph of a triumphant-looking George Lansbury presiding over the sale of much of the British fleet, and the ironically-named London Armaments Treaty of 1938 hung on the opposing wall. Even the official portrait of Anthony Eden, dated January 1939, could not hide the young man's sense of bewilderment. Finally, the half-finished wall in the garden of Downing Street (swiftly demolished by a team from the Reich Engineering Corps) stood as an eerie testament to Britain's last 'democratic' Prime Minister.

The period of British history known as the Second Protectorate by supporters and detractors alike began in March 1941. With the King dead by his own hand (despite what conspiracists still say today, this is the truth of the matter) and the princesses on a submarine in the North Atlantic, the United Kingdom de facto became the Commonwealth of Great Britain (Northern Ireland had been incorporated into O'Duffy's Irish State the month before). Lloyd George (who was at this point not quite the pawn of von Ribbentrop that he would become) was proclaimed Lord Protector by the considerably thinned-out House of Lords.

The Second Protectorate and the horrors that ensued from its rule are well documented elsewhere, so this document will not seek to provide a full picture. But the key events - the appointment of Mosley as Home Secretary in 1942, the Liverpool Rising, the assassination of Seyss-Inquart and resulting annihilation of Godstone - are so etched into any modern Briton's mind that it is surely unnecessary to elucidate much further. For Lloyd George, all this passed as a blur. In 1943, he was forever broken by von Ribbentrop's decision to overrule the National Action Party's 'Police Force (Special Services) Act' and intern the entirety of Britain's constabulary. Mosley proved a greater turncoat even than Lloyd George himself - though his appetite for power shocked the occupiers to the point that they, ironically, blacklisted him from any office higher than the post that was still laughably called 'Home Secretary'.

For the rest of the war, Lloyd George was increasingly used as a figurehead and nothing more. When his health began to seriously wane, he denied even this status. Instead, it would be Harold Nicolson who informed Britons that they had nothing to worry about when Berlin fell in late 1945. The reality of the matter was that, of course, Ribbentrop, Six and other senior officials were frantically loading as much of the Bank of England's gold as they could carry onto ships bound for Argentina.

Lloyd George was barely lucid when London gained the dubious accolade of being the site of the end of the Third Reich. After the formal surrender of London by Generalfeldmarschall Rommel, the last of the eight farcical 'acting Fuhrers', Robert Ley, committed suicide. Rommel immediately asked for passage to Germany in order to establish a transitional government that might restore democracy, but the Red Air Force was, unsurprisingly, unwilling to oblige.

Marshal Slim, commander-in-chief of the British Shock Army for Patriotic Liberation, ordered that 'the Welsh Weasel' be brought to him during the 4th British Rifles' takeover of Whitehall. Two privates allegedly entered the Lord Protector's residence in the basement of Downing Street to find David Lloyd George upright at his desk, but quite dead. Suicide was, remarkably, ruled out, though he had only been dead a few hours.

The man who had led Britain through one national crisis and to destruction during another had left the stage. But, even at that very moment, a plane from Moscow was carrying the man who would play the lead in our nation's next act.

1946-1951 **Stafford Cripps**

Communist Party of the Commonwealth of Great Britain

The son of a Tory and father of a nation

The first man to become First Secretary of the Communist Party of the Commonwealth of Great Britain was, at the time of his birth, the son of a Conservative MP. Born Richard Stafford Cripps in 1889, he embarked on a lengthy intellectual and political journey that began with his father's defection to the Labour Party culminated in his move thoroughly leftwards in the late 1920s.

The Lansbury-era Labour Party was no place for a man of the true left, however, and Cripps became a leading figure in the ever-expanding ILP. A frequent backbench critic of the increasingly pacifistic government, he became an unlikely ally of Winston Churchill, who was grateful to find he was not the only sane man left in Parliament.

When the Eden government collapsed in February 1940, Cripps made an impassioned speech calling for Churchill to be sent for by the King. In return, Churchill made him Minister of Information. Thanks to security protocols making it impossible for Churchill to make a live broadcast, it fell to Cripps to inform the nation via radio that the British Expeditionary Corps had been annihilated at Calais.

Realising that a serious rapprochement with the USSR was the only hope of defeating Hitler, Churchill made Cripps the ambassador to the Kremlin in September 1940. He arrived in the Soviet Union only days before the German invasion of Britain. Immediately upon learning that the Prime Minister was dead, Cripps requested an audience with Stalin himself. This was denied, but the lower-level apparatchiks were just as capable of informing Cripps that he would not receive any support while 'the workers and peasants of the Soviet Union are in alignment with the people of Germany'.

Come May 1941, Cripps' luck changed overnight - along with the luck of many unfortunate Soviet conscripts on the German border. Soon, Cripps had formed the Free British Government (FBG), based in Moscow, and begun regular radio broadcasts critical of the Lloyd George regime. To many, this vaguely aristocratic bureaucrat with a larger-than-life charisma became the unlikely figurehead of British resistance. Ian Fleming (famous to a generation of post-war boys as the inspiration for the dashing and witty resistance hero Jack Flame, scourge of Von Ribbentrop) recalled listening to Cripps' broadcasts with his comrades before going out to wreak havoc with dynamite, farmers' shotguns and pipe-guns (the crude submachine gun design that could be assembled out of essentially anything).

The Free British Government was made up initially of Cripps and his diplomatic staff. Soon, however, the first of the 'Arctic Stowaways' - men fleeing Nazi persecution for their political beliefs - arrived. Clement Attlee, James Maxton and Harry Pollitt had not always seen eye to eye before the war. But now, together with Cripps, they were able to co-operate for the common good.

Help from Moscow's rulers, however, was not forthcoming. This was understandable, as by the autumn of 1941 it looked as though the city would fall by Christmas, and with it, the Soviet war effort. As more and more Arctic Stowaways trickled in, Cripps realised there was something he and the FBG could do to help.

The Cooper-Macmillan regime in Ottawa had gained a deal of legitimacy through the young Queen Elizabeth's 'decision' to reside in Canada, but President Roosevelt sent shockwaves through the 'British establishment' when he declined to formally recognise either the Protectorate, Ottawa or Moscow as the legitimate government of Britain. Sensing an opening, Cripps began to lobby Roosevelt and British escapees in Canada - if they were able to get across the border into the US, it would be theoretically possible for civilian aircraft to fly them to the Russian Far East.

So began the great journey of what would become the British Shock Army.

The first 'Red British' units (as they were affectionately and disparagingly known by Moscow and Ottawa respectively) became operational in the suburbs of Moscow in January 1942. Their war would take them from the Russian capital to the streets of Whitehall, via Kharkov, Minsk, Prague, Vienna and Paris. Their eventual commander, Marshal Slim, decamped from India with the thousands of men he could persuade to embark on the journey that would liberate their homeland - or keep it from harm, in the case of the ethnically Indian troops. So it was that a capital that fell when defended by men from the Home Counties was liberated by men from Newcastle, Toronto and Calcutta.

Cripps was a skilled political operator, and was able to make British liberation a military priority 'as soon as it was viable', after talks with the Soviet politburo. Hours after the celebrations began on Liberation Day, Cripps flew to Croydon Airport (or what was left of it) and held up the red flag.

"I have in my hand a piece of cloth," he said as he descended the steps from the aircraft, "bearing upon it the blood of the workers and soldiers who have slaved for this day. We will remember them - and from the ashes of Nazism, we will build socialism in their name!"

The 'Ottawa Government' was, by this point, a tired irrelevance, and offered loud protests to which no-one paid attention when Cripps called to order the first meeting of the Central Committee of the Communist Party of the Commonwealth of Great Britain (the continued use of the Protectorate-era name was useful for legal, treaty reasons as well as being ideologically acceptable). Cripps, as First Secretary, began the work of government from Britain House, the new name for the rebuilt Senate House, formerly the centre of administration for the University of London.

With Parliament damaged by both bombs and ideological taint (it would reopen as a museum in 1949) and Downing Street out of the question, Cripps made his home in the so-called 'British Kremlin'.

A tireless worker and phenomenally skilled administrator, Cripps regularly went without sleep for days at a time as the country was rebuilt. The Friendship Conference of 1948 saw him at his best, shaking hands with Larkin outside the GPO in Dublin. The enforced 'East Prussia' treatment of Ulster, with Soviet bayonets forcing Unionists onto boats bound for Scotland, was the only controversy of the period of Soviet Occupation. Historians nevertheless hang it around Cripps' neck to this day, and perhaps they are right to do so.

On 1 January 1949, Cripps, flanked by Attlee, Slim, Pollitt, Dutt, Latham and many others, stood on the platform outside Britain House as the occupation force formally withdrew and the CGB was born. As the final tank drove out of sight, Cripps coughed into his handkerchief. Attlee would later record in an interview that 'the flecks of blood I saw then were like daggers in my heart.'

But Cripps still had seventeen months of life in him. He probably would have lived longer if he had not refused to retire. But there was still so much to do. The railway network (particularly in the southeast) was dilapidated and wrecked. Millions of Britons lacked proper homes. Education, a gross parody under Lloyd George, needed outright revolution in light of the brave new world.

Cripps died in his sleep on 1 May 1951. At the May Day parade, his death was announced to tearful crowds and the nation mourned for a week. An unlikely bureaucrat had become an impossible hero - and as Britons stared into the 1950s, a decade of uncertainty stared back. It was, however, tempered by the new European era of brotherhood. From Moscow to Connemara, Narvik to Marseilles, the states of Europe were united - and Britain stood proudly among them.

1951-1968 **Charles Latham**

Communist Party of the Commonwealth of Great Britain

A capital planner

While the Commonwealth mourned its founding father, the manoeuvres to succeed him were already underway. Attlee and Pollitt both fancied the First Secretaryship, but it would be Cripps' favourite assistant, Charles Latham, who took his chair within a month of the old man's untimely death.

One of the most senior figures in the Central Committee not to have been in Moscow during the war, Latham was something of a compromise candidate, and few expected him to last very long. Plans by the Pollitt faction to remove him in the spring of 1953 were put on hold by the death of Stalin, and the backroom chaos that ensued in Moscow led to a firm ruling of 'the status quo is to be preserved' from the Soviet foreign department. It is likely that Latham was aware of the metaphorical stay of execution that he had been granted, for he set about governing much more actively in the mid fifties than he had when he took power.

London was always Latham's first love. He had cut his teeth there as a bureaucrat before the war and got his first job under Cripps as Speaker of the London Assembly (the successor of London County Council). London was in his political blood. In any other period, this may have been problematic, but in the aftermath of the street-fighting (first in 1940, then in 1946) and bombing throughout the war, the capital needed a champion committed to its reconstruction. Cripps had gone some of the way, but Latham ably picked up the torch. British Rail built the North-South Railway (finally creating a single route through London via the use of extensive tunnelling) in record time, though the use of German 'acquired' labour places something of a black mark on this 'miracle of construction'.

London's tram network was reinvigorated, and new power stations were constructed to dampen the impact of the expected (and forthcoming) population boom. The North of England, relatively unscathed during the war, remained an industrial powerhouse and was the most fertile ground in the first Six Year Plan, which had been drafted under Cripps but began under Latham in 1952. Scotland too was in good economic health, and rumblings of separatism had come to an abrupt halt after James Maxton's death and subsequent character assassination on the orders of Moscow. Recently found documents show that so great was the contrast between London and the North at this point, Latham came close to being convinced to move the capital of the CGB to Leeds. What might have happened had he done so is a popular contemplation for counterfactualists.

During the Spanish War of 1955, widely seen as a consolidation move by the ascendant Khrushchev faction in the Kremlin, Latham freely committed British troops to the advance against Franco. When President Dewey caught a whiff that Salazar was next on the agenda, USAGPOR (United States Army Group Portugal) was born and was granted basing rights in the collapsing Portuguese state before one could say 'Azores'. The demilitarised zone around the Spanish-Portuguese border has earned the nickname 'Fortress Iberia', and it is partly through Latham's handiwork. In exchange for the withdrawal of British troops from Spain, he sent ten thousand men's worth of Labour Battalions to the front. To this day, Antwerp Pact forces guarding the border refer to their bunkers as 'Charlies'.

The 1950s were a tumultuous time for the British people. The nationalisation of the Co-operative Wholesale Society led to riots in several major cities and cries of betrayal. Antwerp Pact forces rolled into Amsterdam after anti-Moscow protests in 1958, and the resulting death of

Wagenaar and the imposition of a more doctrinaire Stalinist government seemed to fly in the face of the confusing messages coming from the Kremlin since the Secret Speech of the previous year. J.B. Priestley, Latham's long-serving Secretary of Public Information and chairman of the BBC, was forced out on Moscow's orders in late 1959 after the tone of programming was deemed to be 'incompatible with the workers' state at the present time'. The death of Aneurin Bevan led to another round of public discontent, leading to a terrified Latham telephoning Thorez in Paris and asking for an assurance that troops were not being embarked and sent to Dover. Ironically, to date there is no evidence that Bevan died of anything other than a tragic battle with cancer.

The 'winter of discontent' passed, however, and the 1960s dawned. With them, came a new face in the White House. Beginning one of their dangerous flirtations with hawkishness, Americans elected Joseph 'Joe' Kennedy Jr to the Presidency. A veteran of the American-Japanese War, he had seen the mushroom cloud above Kyoto from his posting on the USS Enterprise. His appetite for nuclear war whetted rather than dampened, he set in motion the events which would culminate in the Azores Missile Crisis.

Latham and Britain played a queer role in the events generally accepted to have been the second closest the world has come to nuclear annihilation. Latham was not like previous leaders of Britain, and this was a good thing - even Cripps would have expected Britain to have been an attending power in any major negotiations about geopolitical matters. The total lack of such an arrangement did not phase the technocratic and small-thinking Latham, who was content with sitting at his desk next to the telephone, waiting to do whatever Nikita Khrushchev required of him. When, in November 1962, it looked like the balloon really was going to go up, all Latham was asked to do was 'make the necessary preparations'.

Those preparations produced a small irony. The emergency broadcasts relating what to do in the event of a nuclear attack were rolled out, and reintroduced viewers to the kindly face and voice of J.B. Priestley, recorded as they were in 1956. Moscow did not seem to care, and thankfully the missiles were gone from the Azores by Advent Sunday - sealing Kennedy's fate as a one-term no-mark.

Latham was shaken but determined to show that Britain's new role in the world - a big island, but no longer a great power - was one of which one could be proud. Production of consumer goods - notably the world famous British Motoring Mini - became the priority, and 'red plenty' the catchphrase of the hour. Rumblings against Khrushchev continued in Moscow, and when the Premier visited London in 1964, he had to cut his visit short to attend a humiliating meeting at which Kosygin and Suslov finally supplanted him. Now having been in office during two transfers of power in Moscow, Latham began to wonder whether he was politically impervious.

Quite obviously, he was not. The 'consumer drive' began to wane in effectiveness, and Soviet defence contractors began to use German steel over British as the Teutonic economy finally kicked back into gear under the tottering Mielke regime. The public even fell out of love with the Mini as its small engine proved woefully unreliable. By 1967, the corridors of Britain House were alive with intrigue as men like James Wilson, Arthur Wicks and the remnants of the faction which had surrounded the late Willie Gallacher sought to use the Mini as a metaphor for Latham's secretaryship. Events intervened one last time - the abortive 'putsch' of January 1968 saw power in Moscow move to Old Bolshevik (and unimpeachable figurehead) Lazar Kaganovich, and 'status quo or face my wrath' became the new order of the day once more.

Latham knew his days were numbered, however, and in more ways than one. His final act before his retirement in the autumn of 1968 was the promotion of his favoured successor - a brilliant, energetic hero of the Great Patriotic War - to the position of First Secretary to the Exchequer. Latham would die less than a year after he left office, but did so a happy and fulfilled man. In the CGB today, he is a moderately divisive figure. Much of his legacy, however, can still be seen in daily life. The Bureau of Statistical Analysis which stands imposingly above the Thames was built under his tenure. The Office of Prices, Quantities and Standards (now Ofspend) was formally inaugurated in 1955. This unassuming technocrat could well have achieved a great deal more in an age of more advanced tabulators. In the time in which he lived, however, he used pen and paper in an attempt to calculate the way toward a better tomorrow.

1968-1969 John Powell

Communist Party of the Commonwealth of Great Britain

Socialism's 'human face'

John Enoch Powell had no interest in politics before the Great Patriotic War. A brilliant classicist and student, he travelled the world and admired the British Empire. The cataclysmic events that would lead to its total destruction could not have been foreseen, but his was a mind that proved capable of changing with the times. His story is one that is as gripping as it is tragic.

Remarkably, an early reference to Powell can be found in the fourth chapter of George Orwell's *London via Vladivostok*, the seminal account of Orwell (real name Eric Blair) and his journey with the men who would become the British Shock Army.

Three days after my arrival at Vladivostok, I was moved into a billet with a larger group of British volunteers. My bed was stiff, small and somewhat damp. To this day, I thank whatever deity may exist for the fact that I somehow did not contract influenza while staying in that rotten place.

The next morning, we were instructed by a commissar in a large woollen hat to go to a large hall, where a soup kitchen had been set up. When I joined the queue for some soup, I became aware that there was a tall man talking loudly to the men either side of him. He had an accent I was unable to place. When I had been handed my bowl of soup, I looked around for him again. He was still talking to his friends. I asked if I might sit at their table.

"Please!" he cried, then continued without a moment's further hesitation, "and as soon as I had made up my mind, I purchased a ticket back to Portsmouth. But not before I had bought a Russian dictionary, mind. I knew then that our fate in this war would depend on them, as it did in 1812 and 1916."

I found him a fiercely impressive, if a little overbearing, individual. I learned he was a classical scholar who had tried to come back to Britain after the war began, but was unable to get a space on any ship headed for the United Kingdom. When he heard what was going on in Vladivostok, he and some others began to lobby for a ship to take them from Sydney. This journey alone warrants a book of its own, and I very much hope he writes it one day.

After that day, we marched to the railway station and began our move west. I spoke with him a few times on the journey, and I hope that what I had to say fascinated him as much as he interested me.

When we reached the front, we were placed in different battalions, and I did not see him again. I later learned he had won two medals, and survived the war.

Orwell died in 1950, with none of his books written after London via Vladivostok being published until long afterwards. It is alleged that a secret copy of The Last Man in Europe made its way to Powell's hands by way of a friend who recognised him from the description. Given Powell's time as First Secretary, it would not be surprising if he had read Orwell's work.

Powell did indeed win two medals - the British People's Medal and the coveted Hero of the Commonwealth of Great Britain. Entering the British Shock Army as a fresh-faced, bookish Private, he ended the war with a slight limp and the rank of Command Brigadier.

After a spell of convalescence in the Lake District, Powell moved to London to assist in the rebuilding of the city. Famously, he worked for two months in a labour gang clearing rubble before his ingenuity was spotted, his war record investigated, and a more suitable job arranged. Finding himself a junior apparatchik in the Office for Prosperity, he came into contact with Charles Latham shortly before the latter secured the top job. Latham saw much potential in Powell, and effectively nurtured his career as his own went from strength to strength. In 1968, he made Powell Secretary to the Exchequer, placing him in overall control of the British economy. When Latham retired four months later, Powell was unanimously elected as his successor by a thoroughly Lathamite Central Committee.

It was an unusually easy transition. The public warmed to Powell immediately, and his first televisual addresses were a first for any nation in the COMECON. "We must give socialism a human face," he was often heard to say, "but it is unfortunate that it should be one as unsightly as mine."

In June 1969, Powell made history again by inviting the underground Liverpudlian music sensation, The Blackjacks, to perform a concert in Hyde Park. The event is commonly believed to have triggered the Summer of London, helped by an unusually hot and sunny spate of weather. Advances in contraception led to a loosening of social norms being more possible. While Powell had no keen interest in such things (besides a passionate desire to end discrimination against homosexuals), he was a keen reformer, cut from far more radical cloth than Latham.

His first target was Britain's mental healthcare. Delivering his famous 'Watertower Speech', he talked of the old Victorian mental 'hospitals' in which the mentally ill and undesirable were locked away. In among his proposals for an end to such outdated and harmful treatments, there was also a hint of something that Kaganovich found unsettling - a subtle suggestion that not everyone currently residing in institutions like Cane Hill was actually mad...

By August, the Summer was in full swing. Obscenity laws had been relaxed to the extent that popular music was now allowed to be, well, popular. Powell and his government, including social reformer Harris Jenkins and industrial democrat Ian Mikardo, pushed on with a series of liberalisations that were presented to the CPCGB at the 21st Party Congress in September. Free speech (already, of course, guaranteed under the Articles of Constitution) was to become a more protected right, as was the freedom of the press. There was a gasp of surprise when Powell, wild-eyed and on powerful form, announced that future elections to the House of the People may 'explore' a multi-party system. This was nothing compared to the stunned, perhaps terrified silence when Powell declared from the podium that, in light of the 'difficult situation in Tajikistan', British troop commitments to the Antwerp Pact were to be 'carefully readdressed'.

Ever since the collapse of the Tajik SSR and the resulting flood of Soviet forces into the region, there had been discontent in the COMECON. Protests, mainly from students, had been protesting 'British boys dying halfway up a mountain on the other side of the globe', while academics and even party officials were uncomfortable with the particular brand of 'brotherhood' that was being shown to people who were nominally citizens of the workers' state. But in essentially putting British withdrawal from the Antwerp Pact - and the Tajik War - on the table, Powell had overplayed his hand. To say nothing of the 'mistake' of calling it Tajikistan, rather than the Tajik SSR...

Within minutes of Powell's speech, telephones were ringing in Moscow, Paris, Berlin and Brussels. The gerontocracies of Europe - Mielke's Germany, Frachon's France and Kaganovich's Russia - united against the frightening, thrusting force that was 'British Socialism'. Two days later, the first Dutch tanks landed at Harwich.

It was an unopposed occupation. Powell knew deploying the New Model Army against the rest of the Antwerp Pact would be suicide, and could lead to a nuclear escalation. Newly-elected President Wallace might as well have had his fingers over his eyes and the song 'Dixie' playing very loudly on a loop when it came to foreign affairs, so any possibility of making the break from Moscow more obvious was non-existent. By the time French T-62s were rolling down London's streets, however (and Czech BMP-1s driving screaming students from Hyde Park), there were those who were willing to fight back.

Students welcomed the tanks with Kaganovich cocktails, and pipe-guns suddenly found themselves in demand once more (though ammunition was in short supply). Passive resistance was a more popular option. The First Secretary of the All-Britain Union of Students, Jack Straw, became a symbol of anti-Soviet feeling when he set himself alight in the midst of a running battle between Belgian forces and British protestors.

The German People's Army was, mercifully, absent from the march on London. The Soviets could see it would not send off the right signals to redeploy the sackers of the city from twenty years earlier. But such matters were of no concern to Powell, who found himself, along with Jenkins and Mikardo, escorted to a transport plane and taken to Moscow on 22 September 1969, where they were forced to sign documents denouncing the actions of the 21st Party Congress and resign all offices of state. In letters published long afterwards, Powell noted that all he had sought to achieve had turned to ash: "Like Virgil and the Tiber, I see the Thames, foaming with much blood." This writing was added to his memorial stone in Highgate last year.

After his political downfall, Powell was granted a dignified but enforced retirement. While Jenkins and Mikardo would in fact return to government in low-level roles in the 1980s, Powell was effectively under house arrest at his home in Birmingham, and passed the time by translating classical poetry and writing endless unsent letters to The Times. He also turned his hand to writing books, none of which were ever published in his lifetime. On his death in 1998, the Office for Cultural Integrity determined that one of his books, a chronicle of his journey from Australia to Russia across the tumultuous Pacific, was publishable. It was called *North through Hell*, and was dedicated to 'a friend, who asked me to write this'.

A complex figure, Powell was not looked upon favourably by the later reformers who had more success than him. Today, he is seen as a reckless ideologue who tried to do too much too soon. Nonetheless, his face, defiant in black, can be seen on many of the blue t-shirts worn by young people today.

1969-1976 Vic Feather

Communist Party of the Commonwealth of Great Britain

Socialism, inaction

"In the long run, we will all be dead." So spoke Vic Feather, First Secretary of the Communist Party of the Commonwealth of Great Britain, in his speech to the 22nd Party Congress.

The quote would come to epitomise the Feather years. A former shop steward, he had fled the 'Labour' Party in disgust during the 1930s and become entrenched in the apparatus of the TUC. After the occupation, one of the first things Franz Six did was try to exterminate the TUC and its apparatus - Feather was one of the Young Turks who went underground and worked with first the Auxiliary Units and then the Red Brigades to keep the idea of solidarity alive through coded messages and a vast underground communications network. Their technology should not be overstated - most 'communications' took place in working men's clubs or pub toilets.

After the internment of all British police officers in 1943, Feather earned a high ranking spot on Six's 'arrest list' when he and others organised the wildcat strike and eventual public disorder that lasted for five days. Already in hiding, the betrayal of a close comrade convinced him he would have to stay quiet for the duration. Feather travelled north, eventually finding work in a Scottish shipyard using forged papers. Four days after Slim made landfall, Feather and a group of his workmates went north to investigate an alleged concentration camp. Linking up with a resistance unit, they eventually found what was left of the now-infamous Gartmore. The guards long gone (most would meet the hangman's noose at Frankfurt), the inmates were starving and in need of serious attention. The emergency efforts to which Feather and his comrades had to go would stay with him for the rest of his life, and instilled in him a powerful dislike of Germans.

After the war, Feather was quickly reinstated in the resurrected TUC. Taking a keen interest in the legislative 'power' this gave him, he became a passionate industrial democrat and worked tirelessly during the 1940s-1950s nationalisations. Singled out for praise at the end of the second six year plan, he was promoted to become a permanent member of the Central Committee.

Feather's war experiences, along with his drive for workplace rights, made him one of the earlier converts to the Moscow way of doing things. By the end of the 1960s, he was a staunch supporter of the party line, and a regular stonewaller at Central Committee meetings when disputes with the Soviet Union were being discussed. Harris Jenkins, before the untimely end of his career, described him as "one of those men who becomes more authoritarian with age."

During the Summer of London, Feather deliberately kept himself out of sight. He quietly voted against the liberalisations passed at the 21st Party Congress, and made himself scarce during eventual Antwerp Pact invasion. Legend has it that he commandeered a taxi all the way to his office in London as soon as he heard that Powell had been airlifted out of the country. Sure enough, when he arrived, the phone was ringing.

His 'election' as First Secretary was rather more of an installation than those of his predecessors. He was not a popular choice among a Central Committee that was still relatively liberal-minded. Feather soon found a solution to that - the 'Polite Purge' of 1970 saw the committee restocked with hardliners and loyalists, and a platform of 'consolidation' pursued on all fronts.

Feather's time in office is often described as so spectacularly boring that it is forgotten about by all but the most committed students of history. This is not strictly true, and a little unfair on a man who led a fascinating life. There is, however, no denying the fact that Feather was not a transformative leader. During his seven year rule, British Motors nearly collapsed and was saved via a loan from Moscow (and stopped exporting to the continent until the early 1990s), house-building remained steady, defence spending mildly increased (the Cromwell V tank rolled past Britain House for the first time under Feather), and civil liberties became virtually non-existent.

Dissent was harshly cracked down upon by the increasingly 'paternal' Feather, who argued again and again that the pursuit of long term goals was pointless - socialism was in the here and now, and while future generations might benefit and build something more, the priority of the people's state must be the welfare of the people, and the socialist right of each man to gain fulfilment - material and spiritual - from his labour.

Those who did not agree with this to the letter (or, more accurately, those who thought the government was making a pig's ear of things) were strictly punished. Tom Stoppard, ironically a refugee from Nazi persecution, had his entire catalogue blacklisted and was himself sentenced to five years in Belmarsh after Hugh Scanlon recognised a less-than-subtle caricature in his 1974 play Paradise. Richard Ingrams was sent to the Isle of Wight after James Wilson objected to a mock interview that was published in an unlicensed satirical journal, *Policeman*. And these are merely the more 'glamorous' examples. Thousands of Britons were imprisoned during this period, some simply for questioning the competence of particularly influential and vindictive regional administrators.

Internationally, Feather had a simple approach - keep Britain's nose clean. As the Tajik War intensified, British troop commitments were increased, but when things looked as though they might get 'problematic' again, the war came to an abrupt end. Brutal reprisals and a policy of 'if you associate with these people, we will kill you' had finally won. The Tajik SSR was formally reincorporated into the Soviet Union, and hundreds of British servicemen returned home to a life of permanent mental scarring.

When Denmark had its own brush with reformism under Jorgensen in 1973, Feather famously cancelled a scheduled visit to Copenhagen. The tanks did not end up rolling in on this occasion, as Jorgensen was 'quietly persuaded to retire' by his panicking comrades in the DKP.

The only occasion on which Feather was at all present in international affairs was at the funeral of President Wallace later that year. An unguarded comment to an accompanying aide about 'reaping the whirlwind of slavery' led to an immediate re-frosting of Anglo-American relations when it was plastered all over the US papers.

Vic Feather was First Secretary of the Communist Party of the Commonwealth of Great Britain for seven years. All things considered, it is impossible to say whether he did badly or whether he did well. The general malaise of the early-1970s COMECON economic performance, exacerbated by the 1974 Yom Kippur War, can hardly be laid at his door. And when one is a slave to masters in another land, can one truly be held responsible for one's decisions? When he died suddenly in office in 1976, a cruel joke circulated the pubs of Britain: "It's the first thing he's done in years…"

1976-1984 Max Levitas

Communist Party of the Commonwealth of Great Britain

From Cable Street to the Central Committee

A communist stalwart born to Baltic Jewish parents in London's East End, Max Levitas was at Cable Street when Mosley and his thugs tried to march through. When the actual Nazis arrives four years later, Levitas joined the resistance, first as a deliverer of underground newspapers. By the end of the war, he was blowing up railways with the Molotov Club.

A plain-speaking man with simple roots, Levitas served as a useful counterweight to the more intellectual occupants of the Central Committee. When the Chinese Scare of 1971 had various more bookish figures in the government on edge, it was Levitas who persuaded them there was no risk of 'another Azores' because the Chinese simply had 'nowhere else to go'. Sure enough, by the end of the year, Lin was reassured, calmer, and in control of the party and of China. Relations with the Kremlin normalised, and the Indian government in particular breathed a sigh of relief.

Levitas cut his teeth on foreign affairs in the former Raj. In 1959, he was made ambassador to the Balaram government and was present during the renewal of the Indo-Soviet 'treaty of friendship' that had been in place since the death of Lloyd George. Finding the climate delightful but the work uninspiring, Levitas requested a transfer into a domestic department in 1963, and by the mid-sixties he was the Assistant Secretary for Prices, Quantities and Standards. In 1967, he was made Secretary for Housing and Civil Construction, partnering him with the brilliant Rodney Gordon. Gordon's brutalist designs were revolutionising inner London and would, across the next fifteen years, become a common (if divisive) sight in all major cities of the CGB.

By 1976, Levitas was a powerful and respected member of the Central Committee. On Feather's sudden death, he was the obvious candidate to replace him. Brushing aside a nominal challenge from Jack Jones (who was, in 1977, sent to oversee tyre production in Brentford), Levitas took over the CGB in the bloodless fashion the country had become used to. It might not have been so easy - when his candidacy was first considered, there was an elephant in the room that made some Secretaries uneasy. Levitas was Jewish. Were it not for the fact that the leader of the Soviet Union himself was as well, it is unlikely that this 'landmark moment' for British Jews would have occurred. As it happened, even the most strident anti-Semites in the government could barely talk higher than a whisper while Kaganovich was still in charge. When the Grand Old Man stood down in 1978, Levitas was already entrenched and had, thankfully, weeded out the more reactionary members of the Central Committee.

While he shared Feather's desire for stability and prosperity, Levitas was aware of the dangers of appearing to govern as a do-little. While 'public discontent' was hardly the concern it had been in the days of 'democracy', a riot at the wrong time could lead to a telephone call from Moscow and a one-way ticket to a farm in Wales.

With this in mind, Levitas made himself a very public figure. 'Dynamic socialism' became the watchword of the day, and the BBC had its Expectations Charter for 1975-1980 formally ripped up and replaced with a new, more targeted agenda. Levitas allowed the Central Committee to become perceived as slightly more 'human' and 'in touch'. They were present, for example, at the FA Cup final in 1978, (where Portsmouth Maritime beat Watford 3-2). The nightly news began to feature the relevant secretaries reading out statements themselves (in the style, though not the reality, of an interview) rather than simply sending a fax of what to say straight to the BBC.

Critics have called Levitas' tenure 'window dressing'. Real reform was not forthcoming, but the Cable Street veteran did a very good job of making people feel like things were substantially better than they had been. In many ways, it was an impossible task to meaningfully reform the British state within ten years of the Summer of London.

The 'window dressing' charge is, however, somewhat unfair. There was a small but noticeable relaxation of public censorship, though only in the fields of 'entertainment'. Shakespeare, as in the Soviet Union, had never been censored and had for years served as the obvious outlet for subversive directors and actors. Peter Hall's 1980 Hamlet, starring Derek Jacobi, turned Elsinore into an ever-watching police state, and contained sequences all too familiar to Britons who had been present when Special Branch raided or shut down a pub.

Hall's production was not a new phenomenon - as early as 1960, Laurence Olivier directed a seminal Measure for Measure, and allowed the idea of a benevolent ruler disguising himself and going among his people in order to survey them to speak for itself. Olivier was visited at his home by Special Branch, it is alleged, but no formal action was taken.

What made the 1980 Hamlet so significant was what followed it. After three extended runs at the People's Theatre and a trip to Broadway (the 'Muskie Thaw' was in full swing), there was a palpable sense that the Levitas regime was becoming more permissive in terms of culture. It is this mood that inspired Harold Pinter to write (or rather, put on - he had written it in the 1960s) The Birthday Party a confusing, savage play that involved two men breaking down an apparently innocent man through interrogation. When, in 1982, it was a rave success, Levitas was faced with a choice. In a move that would define his cultural legacy, he contacted British Films and asked that Mr Pinter be contacted about a screenplay of the work.

While foreign affairs were never his strength, relations with the German Democratic Republic were particularly strained during Levitas' tenure. He found it impossible to hide his disdain for his comrades in Berlin. While this was understandable given the fate of several members of his family during the war (including his older brother), it seriously damaged his position and credibility as Germany gained the ascendancy within the western end of the COMECON. In an example of this attitude leaking into the British bureaucracy at large, a small international incident occurred as a result of a British couple being detained for two months by Special Branch on their return from a motorcycle holiday in the GDR. In an ugly reminder of attitudes officially buried under Socialism, many commented in private that there would have been no suspicion of 'treachery' or 'deviance' if the two youngsters were not a mixed race couple.

'Temper the Teutons' had been the unofficial slogan of the British government since the war, echoing the attitude pursued by Moscow. But the 'post-war trudge' that had eventually brought German industry back up to speed by the mid-1960s was impossible to reverse. To dismantle one generation of factories and rebuild them in other countries is unfortunate - to dismantle two is sheer malice.

The backwards-looking nature of French socialism also meant that France began to fall significantly behind both Britain and Germany. Unwilling to change (or perhaps unable to), and hamstrung by strikes and the rise of the illegal Solidarité trade union, the French state had a difficult 1970s. By the end of the decade, rumblings were afoot of a military takeover on Moscow's orders, and sure enough by 1981 General Archambault was 'President and Defence Secretary of the People's Republic'.

The economic turmoil of the mid-1970s was weathered rather more effectively by the British people, however - a new generation of folk songs, akin to those sung in air raid shelters, would be heard cheerily ringing out from queues for bread, fuel or appliances. The Mini, its engine slightly improved, became a beloved symbol of Self-Sustaining Economics, Levitas' favourite slogan. The usual waiting lists for the Mini came down to below six months for the first time in 1981. It seemed things were on the up.

Sadly for a man who focused his life on Britain, it would be foreign affairs that ended Levitas' life. He attended the January 1984 Ankara Conference, at which both Tikhonov and Muskie agreed to a reduction in nuclear warheads. Allegedly a last-minute intervention from him saved the whole deal from collapse, though it is unknown how much of that claim is after-the-fact hagiography. Desperate to get home, he boarded the BOA flight back to Croydon International airport. Somewhere over the Adriatic, the plane broke apart and he was killed along with four other senior Central Committee members - and thirty others.

An inquiry was immediately launched into the crash, but no evidence of foul play was ever found. To this day, however, there are those who curse Koliševski and his government for an alleged missile strike on the aircraft. While foul play was never formally proven, the crash sparked the series of events that would lead to the occupation of Yugoslavia and full incorporation into COMECON and Antwerp by 1988.

As for Max Levitas, he is fondly remembered by many in Britain today. A cheerier face than Feather before him, and the last of Britain's leaders to have actively fought in the war or resistance, his abrupt passing represented a sea change in British governance. As 1984 dawned, Britons wondered what awaited them next.

1984-1990 Jimmy Reid

Communist Party of the Commonwealth of Great Britain

The nation's big brother

Socialism in the British Isles had always owed a great deal of its heritage to Scotland. That no Scot had yet led the Commonwealth of Great Britain became something of a hot-button issue in the early 1980s, with Scottish oil now being drilled up and Max Levitas looking as though he would go on until at least the year 2000. The 1984 air crash intervened, however, and when the decapitated Central Committee met to discuss the leadership transition, the Secretary for Transport & Maritime Affairs was able to play on the Celtic sympathies of the meeting to get himself elected as its chair. The following Friday, Peter Cook announced on the BBC News at Eight that James 'Jimmy' Reid had become Britain's first Scottish First Secretary.

Reid was born in Govan in 1932, and at the age of 15 was already working in the Clyde shipyards. The shift of Britain from imperial power to modest nation state had surprisingly little bearing on her shipbuilding - with no fleet to speak of after 1946, the construction of the small but effective People's Navy kept the Clyde a flurry of activity up until the late 1950s. By then, merchant traffic was in high demand as lucrative trade agreements with the COMECON-'friendly' nations like India, Indonesia and China required a vast building programme for the Prosperity Fleet (formerly the Merchant Navy).

Reid began work in 1947 and by the age of 18 was a shop steward. He once shook hands with a visiting Stafford Cripps, and determined on that day that he would one day hold the same office. By 1969, he was the youngest ever Administrative Secretary for the 'Region' of Scotland. It was a nomenclature to which he strongly objected, but he was now the most powerful central government figure north of the 'border'.

Reid was long-serving in that post, overseeing the north of Scotland's transition into an industrial powerhouse, earning him the nickname 'the butcher of the cottage industries'. His first love was always shipping, and in the aftermath of Vic Feather's death, he was made Secretary for Transport & Maritime Affairs, a national post he had long craved.

Nakedly careerist and a formidable debater, he toured Scotland when oil was discovered in the North Sea and made a number of speeches that earned him the ire of Moscow's watchful eye. Wary of a 'highland Tajikistan', Levitas talked him down and 'suggested' he focus on rejuvenating the flagging rail network, whose High Speed Link project had stalled for several years.

Reid proved capable enough at getting that project off the ground, though he courted controversy when German engineers were invited to come and oversee the construction of the new route, effectively a re-opening of the 'Grand Central'.

Railway locomotives were one of the few things Britain unquestionably led the COMECON in. The brutal 'Continental Loading Gauge Or Bust' programme of the late 1950s (overseen by the uncompromising and driven Richard Beeching) had brought Britain into line with most of Europe by demolishing and rebuilding hundreds of bridges and tunnels, as well as widening the gap between tracks around the country. The disruption this caused lasted six years, but the higher capacity that it made possible made it all worthwhile.

Reid, therefore, inherited a modern railway that was trying to become more up-to-date. Deltics purred across Europe, hauling trains from Calais to Warsaw, and British Locomotion had a rightful place at the top of the informal 'aristocracy of labour' that came to be among Britain's working men and women.

Having made a name for himself in this capacity, he was an acceptable choice to many, particularly Scots, when he took power in 1984. His six-year tenure, however, would be marked by scandal and disagreement with Moscow.

In 1986, a major collapse at the Ellington Colliery killed 94 men. Reid immediately travelled to the scene, but it quickly became clear that severe safety failures were responsible. The trail eventually led to the Secretary for Mining, Mick McGahey. With no free press, the matter remained internal to the Party, but Reid was placed under significant pressure to sack his friend. Each day that he did not, rumours circulated of a 'Caledonian mafia' in Britain House. Eventually, McGahey was 'moved' to a position overseeing experimental desalination plants on the west coast of Scotland, but Reid had already been irreparably damaged.

On Christmas Day, 1986, Tikhonov was finally outmanoeuvred and the 'reform faction' took its long-awaited place as the ascendancy in Moscow. There was some dispute as to who would become General Secretary, but eventually Grigory Romanov became the first leader of the Soviet Union to have been actually born in the Soviet Union. As if overnight, Reid's star began to fall.

It would still take three years for the knives to be sharpened, however. Reid's reputation as a Feather-esque do-nothing had become dangerous, and allegations of cronyism and corruption were widespread within the party. By contrast, he was ruthless at controlling public opinion and was hugely popular and, at least ostensibly, adored by the masses. He seemed completely irremovable, a status apparently cemented by the enthusiastic invitation he received to join the embraces on the pitch when Great British captain Peter Shilton held the World Cup above his head at Wembley in 1988.

But nothing lasts forever. Eventually, a poisonous campaign of manipulated press appearances and anonymous letters in The Times began to discredit Reid. Finally, the long-serving Secretary for Technology, Anthony

'Tony Benn' Wedgwood-Benn, moved a motion to remove him in a meeting in the spring of 1990. Wedgwood-Benn was a passionate reformer and had been very nearly arrested and blacklisted in 1969. Obsessed with tabulators and the role they had to play in 'the coming shtate of full Communishum', he was seen as a little odd by his comrades. Nonetheless, his vote carried and he found himself chairing the Central Committee meeting to elect Reid's successor.

However, if Wedgwood-Benn had hoped to stay there for long, he was disappointed. A backroom deal, long-arranged and now brought into play, removed him within forty-eight hours, and on 4 April 1990 the people of the CGB had a new leader - one that did not intend to be removed for a very long time.

1990-2008 **Ken Livingstone**
Communist Party of the Commonwealth of Great Britain
Millennium Man

Not since Charles Latham had London known a more permanent presence than Ken Livingstone. Born in Lambeth during the Great Patriotic War, he was first elected to the London Assembly in 1969 by subtly appearing to endorse the Summer of London and then loudly condemning it when the wind changed. A veteran of the capital's politics, he became the LA's Speaker in 1980 and became a Visiting Member of the Central Committee in this capacity. Wasting no time, he formed alliances with key figures that would come to serve him well ten years later.

Expertly removing Wedgwood-Benn after using him as a blunt instrument to remove Reid, Livingstone set about consolidating his power base. Friendly to reform for as long as Moscow required him to be, one of his first moves was to announce the relaxation of press controls in a remarkably candid interview with Peter Cook on the BBC in 1991. As the British economy flourished in the 1990s boom, the new Soviet policies of 'openness' and 'restructuring' were praised for the rise in consumer goods that were flooding out of the bloc's major production centres in Birmingham, Belgrade, Berlin, Stalingrad and elsewhere.

Livingstone's style of governance relied on placing himself at the heart of everything good that happened, and finding scapegoats to sack when things went wrong. It was something he was remarkably effective at - he ruthlessly ended Peter Purves' career when educational standards were found to be slipping. After a massaging of the figures the following year, the front page of The Times was covered with images of attractive young students and Ken Livingstone. When the New Mini proved a dismal failure, he was nowhere to be found, but after the launch of the Mini Two in 1995, he was seen driving one whenever he needed a car.

This was not often - one thing Livingstone was apparently sincere about was his desire to be a 'man of the people'. As a result, he used public transport wherever possible, and was passionate about its reform. Later in his tenure, he would introduce the Liberty Card, which allowed for 'touch-in, touch-out' use of trains and buses around the CGB, with money deducted directly from one's Bank of Britain account.

The 1990s were a healing period for Europe. A visit from Clement XV to Paris in 1993 was a sign that the shadow of the Archambault years had finally passed. General Secretary Sartre (a distant relative of the philosopher) had made his start in the Solidarité union, and the increased level of autonomy he and his government had been granted boded well for the rest of the COMECON. Livingstone in particular was grateful for the opportunity to create even more of a cult of personality.

When President Biden made his landmark visit to London in 1996, 'Kenmania' reached new heights. Huge images of Livingstone hung from anywhere that could hold them, his preferred picture being of him in casual shirtsleeves and a loosened tie. It was the face of a modern man of the people, who wanted prosperity for his family and his fellow man.

The fiftieth anniversaries - of the end of the war in 1996, and the CGB's birth in 1999 - were masterfully-executed displays of propaganda. Shockingly, Powell's tenure as First Secretary was explored in documentaries and public exhibitions for the first time during the 1999 celebrations. The new Moscow doctrine of 'loosening' had been welcomed by Livingstone, and the cautious examination of Powell was a test of the water. When red helicopters failed to appear above London, many countries around the COMECON began to pull softly away from Moscow's party line but remained fully committed to the economic and military relationship they had with the Soviet Union and their neighbouring states.

As 1999 went by, Britons looked toward the new millennium. Livingstone was thrilled at the opportunity to stage-manage another grand event, but was wise enough not to place himself at its heart. A celebration under the name 'a thousand years of Britain' made a mockery of serious history but placed the working man at the centre of every event since the Battle of Hastings. It proved incredibly successful. More controversial was Livingstone's announcement that William Bragg, one of Britain's foremost State Musicians, would be rewriting the lyrics of 'Our Commonwealth', the national anthem. While some changes were accepted as necessary updates ('every man' became 'everyone' in the first verse), Bragg was unable to go as far as he liked. 'We look not to Kings or Emperors' remains – 'We don't need a King or Emperor' was a colloquialism too far.

Elsewhere in the cultural world, Harold Pinter, by now artistic director of the People's Theatre, produced another series of controversial plays that 'questioned' the heavy-handedness of Soviet rule in the pre-1986 era. Livingstone himself attended the 2003 production of *Shit Happens* by Stafford Hare.

One thing Livingstone had not counted on having to deal with was the rise of the 'international network' (soon abbreviated to internet). First developed by COMECON scientists looking to share data easily between countries, by 1995 'town halls' were becoming increasingly popular with those who had access to a tabulator and a phone line. The age of the personal tabulator dawned in 2000, appropriately, with the Soyutab III becoming the first model affordable to most European citizens. Livingstone was wary, along with Gorbachev in Russia (who had taken over from Romanov in January). Total freedom of communication was, in theory, vital to the achievement of full Communism. But in practice, after the first 'online organised' public disturbance in Bradford, the 'internet' became heavily controlled. A new department of Special Branch was established, and soon its less-than-subtle observers became nicknamed 'trolls' for their attempts to entrap users into revealing sensitive information and unacceptable opinions.

In the United States, Rockefeller was trying his best to oversee a millennial boom of his own, without much success. The reduction in possible exports to Asia after the inevitable 1997 revolution in Japan exacerbated the already chilly relationship with a China that finally joined the COMECON in 1999. One saving grace for the Americans was their telecommunications technology. 'Amerinet' proved more popular than the 'internet' thanks to its lack of controls or spies.

In 2005, Livingstone welcomed the first import of American goods to Britain. Rockefeller had been defeated in a landslide, and the 'pro-conciliation, pro-reality' candidate, Ron Paul, had ushered in a new era of free trade with the COMECON. Gorbachev was only too happy to oblige, feeling that by this point the socialist juggernaut of Russo-Franco-Germano-Anglo-Italo-Sino-Indian strength could handle the pressure of being compared to a more decadent way of producing consumer goods.

By 2006, Livingstone was feeling tired. It is perhaps typical of his leadership style that when he pondered, for a moment, who might succeed him, he could see no-one. It was true that he had crushed the careers and credibility of anyone who might have stood a chance of supplanting him. Herbert Mandelson was the last to go, forced out after an explosion at a fertiliser plant he had allegedly signed off as 'modern and safe'. Aware his health was struggling - though he was only 61 - Livingstone pushed on, determined to find and groom a successor.

He would not eventually find one. In 2008, shortly after overseeing the hugely successful 9th Internationalist Games in London, Livingstone suffered a minor heart attack and realised he could no longer go on. Resigning in the knowledge that his likely successor would be a non-entity was hard for him, but he had his achievements to cheer himself up. He had inherited a Commonwealth struggling to find a place in a post-authoritarian world. By displaying his own brand of personal authority, he had shown Britons one way forward, at least.

In modern polling, Livingstone regularly finishes alongside Cripps as Britons' favourite leader since the war. Today, he lives in Highgate with his collection of amphibians.

2008-2015 **Michael Sugar**
Communist Party of the Commonwealth of Great Britain
A man in need of an apprentice

As Livingstone fired everyone who had an ounce of leadership potential in them, when his unplanned retirement went ahead he found no-one with credibility to succeed him remained in the Central Committee. Michael Sugar, the Secretary for Technology, easily filled the void by being the 'least bad' choice of a committee well aware of their own weaknesses (though a vain attempt to secure the leadership by Alan Titchmarsh still took place).

What can one say about Michael Sugar? Despite his later reputation as a gruff, boring technocrat, his youth was anything but. Born to Jewish parents in the East End in 1947, his family had spent the war in hiding. Growing up, he joined the Angry Young Men in their hunt for Nazis that had gone unpunished, eventually playing a part in John Osborne's capture of Otto Frank. Frank's trial in the Levantine Republic in 1968 shaped Sugar's commitment to justice.

Unsurprisingly, his political idol was Max Levitas. When the latter pinned a medal on his chest, he called the event the proudest day of his life - it remained as such. Finding the corridors of power open to him in the early 1980s, he joined the Office for Technology and became an effective manager of tabulator experts, eventually gaining some skills himself.

By the 1990s, he was overseeing the internet in the CGB. It was this element of his 'CV' that probably got him the top job in 2008 - he was the only member of the committee with any experience of dealing with a concrete example of the modern, changing world. His first action as First Secretary was to take part in a live netchat with Mumsnet, signalling a more open government than Livingstone's. The chat was a disaster, however, as Sugar was uncomfortable with the scrutiny on display, and the experience made him cautious about further attempts at such things.

When Ivanov took over the politburo in the summer of 2008, many in the CPCGB had begun to sing 'the people's flag is palest pink'. Sugar was less concerned - he was always results-driven, rather than interested in ideology. The proposals coming out of Moscow of 'multi-party, single goal' elections were met with jubilation by many liberal Britons, though many were disappointed by the imposition of an Office for Multiparty Ideology that ensured right-wing or 'deviant' policies would not be granted a platform. Sugar agreed to the plans, and in 2011 announced the first 'free' elections in the CGB would take place in 2016.

This was essentially the last interesting thing Sugar did. Various failed attempt to 'tabulatorise' NHS records, criminal records and industrial quotas popped up in headlines from time to time, but by and large Britons were able to get on with their lives in the knowledge that someone in Britain House was probably doing something, but they didn't know what it was. In many ways, this was perhaps a good thing by accident - the totalitarian era of the 'cold war' was well and truly over, and some waggish 'political scientists' celebrated the news that name recognition of Central Committee members was at an all time low.

The power of regional administrators waned as well under Sugar. Not because power was being centralised, but because their authority was simply less relevant these days. People's 'buying power' had increased, shortages were a rarity, and so the usual peacekeeping and (metaphorical) firefighting that local Administrative Secretaries had to do in the past was no longer necessary.

Sugar seemed to get bored with power very quickly. As Britons enjoyed cuisines and clothing they had only ever dreamt of, he seemed to miss a simpler time when he was able to be one of the people. He made it his priority to fill the Central Committee with brilliant younger men and women than himself, so that he could retire safe in the knowledge that the country would be in competent hands.

"This is not an age for great minds," he would often say, "but for great brains." He knew the value of tabulators in calculating a planned economy, and was often modest about his role in overseeing year-on-year growth in both consumer goods production and industrial products. After eighteen months of surrounding himself with bright young things (and occasionally getting in trouble for his backwards attitudes to gender), Sugar made a shock announcement in his 2014 Christmas address to the nation - that he would resign early in the new year. It is too soon to properly assess what his legacy will be, but it is likely that the history books will not remember Michael Sugar for much - in politics, at least.

2015-present **Nicola Sturgeon**
Communist Party
The first lady

Nicola Sturgeon appeared at first to be an astonishing choice for First Secretary. But her story, in many ways, has made her rise inevitable. Born in 1970 to an electricians' shop steward and a dentist, she first entered politics when, as a District Fellow for the Federation of Woodcraft Folk, she was sent as a delegate to London to speak at Cripps Memorial Central Hall in Westminster. Addressing the 1986 Conference of Organisations, she spoke to applause of the prosperity the latest six year plan had to her fellow Woodcraft Folk, and their families, in Scotland. Managing then to include a coded criticism of the government's fisheries policy was more impressive, but attracted no public acclaim. She was 'noticed' however, and while her fate would have been a simpler and more brutal affair a mere decade earlier, she found herself instead earmarked for promotion into the civil service as soon as her studies were over.

After earning a degree in Administration from Leeds Technical Institute (where her forthright speaking style earned her the nickname 'Nikita'), she was approached by the government and invited to assume the post that had been readied for her. Once again, Sturgeon rebelled. Politely, as always, she insisted at the age of 22 that she would not be content performing 'data entry' into the tabulators of the Office for Public Health. Incredibly, she was listened to once again, and became Britain's youngest Industrial Organiser when she was sent to Aberdeen to oversee a section of the Maclean Pipeline. By the end of her twenties, she was Under-Secretary for Oil, answering only to Brian Souter. When the latter was softly purged during Sugar's ascent to power, Sturgeon entered the Central Committee in her former superior's old job, earning the nickname 'the woman in black'.

Sturgeon appears to have grown tired of oil at this point, and made a further reputation for herself under Sugar as Secretary for the Media from 2009. Liberalising a number of press regulations and joining Norway and Wallonia in legalising 24-hour 'rolling news' channels, Sturgeon was a British foil to the dynamic General Secretary Ivanov in Russia. Her reputation with the public maintained by a grateful (and more powerful) press, Sturgeon was easily able to move sideways to the head of the new Office for Multiparty Ideology in 2011. The emergence of the Industrial Democrats, Britain's first new (legal) political party in half a century, proved a success, and so the Agrarian Union and PEACE (Powellites and Egalitarians for Action on Climate and Ecology) followed. In 2014, she earned the ire of her home nation by blocking the approval of a 'Scottish Party'. "When the Commonwealth is socialist, nationalism is a path toward only one thing," she said darkly. Similar regional parties were rejected throughout her tenure at OfMI.

By the time Sugar retired, Sturgeon had overseen the creation, vetting and staffing of eight different political parties, and had travelled to observe the elections in Italy, Croatia-Slavonia, and the Trieste Republic. It was from this springboard that Sturgeon was able to make her passionate pitch to the Central Committee of the Communist Party of the Commonwealth of Great Britain. "Make me First Secretary," she doubtless said, "for I'm the only one of you who knows how to be a party leader as well as a national one."

The vote was narrower than it could have been. Sturgeon's naked ambition has always intimidated other members of the Central Committee, and on this occasion it was almost enough to put Chris Kendall, another youngster but a far more traditional Party figure, into the First

Secretary's chair. But Sturgeon won the day, allegedly thanks to a last minute deal with a power-bloc on the Committee itself.

Sturgeon took office on May Day 2015. A fresh-faced and open relationship with the media has ensued, with Sturgeon always responding to the accolade "the first woman First Secretary" with "but the second Scot". Her first major act was to rename the CPCGB simply 'the Communist Party', an act which was accompanied by a number of 'rebrands' in preparation for 2016's elections. At present, the Communist Party is expected to easily win a majority in the House of the People, and not just thanks to the automatic weighting given to the Communists by the new 'Preferential Voting' system. Sturgeon is genuinely popular, and while she declined TV debates (pointing to the chaos that had unfolded live when the First Secretary of Germany had simply refused to answer any questions from his 'impudent' challengers), she made good use of the provisions laid out in the Allotted Television Time (Governing Parties) Act of 2014.

With the New Constitution now passed into law, it is almost beyond doubt that the people of Britain will elect Nicola Sturgeon as their first 'Premier' in next year's election. The question then will be simple. Where will she take them next?

Appendix A

Flag of the Commonwealth of Great Britain, 1946-present

Appendix B

Europe at the present time (c.2015)

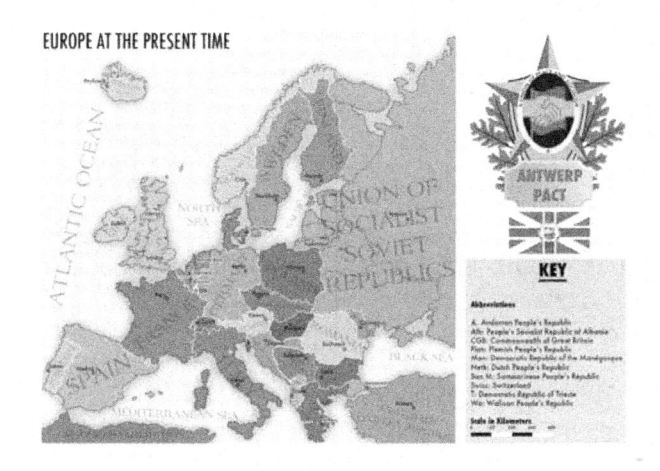

Appendix C

National anthem of the Commonwealth of Great Britain
Melody by Gustav Holst, lyrics by GDH Cole (revised in 1999 by William Bragg)

Our Commonwealth is yours and mine, our neighbours' and our friends'.
Built on comradeship and common good; on which we can depend.
Our factories are ours, our harvests are our own,
Thanks to friendship and labour, no Briton stands alone.
There is wealth, but there's no decadence: everyone shall have their share,
And the old, the sick, and vulnerable shall never want for care.

We look not to Kings or Emperors, no sovereigns rule here.
We are side by side as socialists, and free from want and fear.
Through partnership in Europe, through trade across the Earth,
We can share our prosperity and prove our people's worth.
Gone are days of slaves and colonies, goodbye to Lords and Earls.
Britons stand as noble equals, to any in the world!

We have built another country, where all of us are free.
A land where men and women are counted equally.
Children learn and play together, workers all succeed as one,
Over poverty and ignorance, the victory is won.
As the future stretches out ahead, our hopes only increase,
As we live in leftist brotherhood, and everlasting peace.

Appendix D

Leaders of the United Kingdom (1801-1941) and Commonwealth of Great Britain (1941 – present)

1935 – 1939: George Lansbury (Labour)
1939 – 1940: Anthony Eden (Conservative)
1940: Winston Churchill (Conservative leading Wartime Coalition) †
1940 – 1946: David Lloyd George (National Action) †
1946 – 1951: Stafford Cripps (CPCGB) †
1951 – 1968: Charles Latham (CPCGB)
1968 – 1969: John Powell (CPCGB)
1969 – 1976: Vic Feather (CPCGB) †
1976 – 1984: Max Levitas (CPCGB) †
1984 – 1990: Jimmy Reid (CPCGB)
1990 – 2008: Ken Livingstone (CPCGB)
2008 – 2015: Michael Sugar (CPCGB)
2015 – present: Nicola Sturgeon (CPCGB)

Leaders of the Union of Soviet Socialist Republics (1917 – present)

1926 – 1953: Joseph Stalin (CPSU) †
1953 – 1964: Nikita Khrushchev (CPSU)
1964 – 1968: Alexei Kosygin (CPSU)
1968 – 1978: Lazar Kaganovich (CPSU)
1978 – 1986: Nikolai Tikhonov (CPSU)
1986 – 2000: Grigory Romanov (CPSU)
2000 – 2008: Mikhail Gorbachev (CPSU)
2008 – present Sergei Ivanov: (CPSU)

Presidents of the United States of America (1776 – present)

1933 – 1945: Franklin Delano Roosevelt (Democratic)
1945 – 1948: Henry Wallace (Democratic)
1949 – 1957: Thomas Dewey (Republican)

1957 – 1961: Henry Cabot Lodge, Jr (Republican)
1961 – 1965: Joseph P. Kennedy Jr (Democratic)
1965 – 1969: Nile Kinnick (Republican)
1969 – 1973: George Wallace (Democratic) †
1973 – 1977: Terry Sanford (Democratic)
1977 – 1981: Nelson Rockefeller (Republican)
1981 – 1989: Edmund Muskie (Democratic)
1989 – 1993: Robert Redford (Democratic)
1993 – 2001: Joseph Biden (Republican)
2001 – 2009: David Rockefeller Jr (Democratic)
2009 – present: Ron Paul (Republican)

Finally, the question of what happened to the royal family in Canada. Canada voted to become a republic in 1961, and as Princess Elizabeth was never crowned, few people actually consider her Queen. The Empire collapsed into Soviet-dominated African states and a very COMECON-friendly India, so there really wasn't much need for a Queen (or Empress) anymore. As such, Princess Elizabeth quietly changed her official style to Lady Elizabeth Windsor in the 1970s. On her death in 2022, her eldest son Louis confirmed he wished to continue living as a private Canadian citizen.

Afterword

Since I first came across alternate history, I have been fascinated by the possibilities presented by altered paths for ideologies. Did neoliberalism have to dominate the late-20th century? Was fascism the only force that could have started the Second World War, and was it necessarily doomed by its defeat in that conflict? And – like many in Western countries – I wondered what my own homeland would look like under a red flag.

Meet The New Boss was born from a desire to explore not the well-trodden ground of a 'home-grown' left wing Britain. There are many works that do this already, including the excellent *Fight and Be Right* and *The World of Fight and Be Right* by Ed Thomas, which I heartily recommend. But this story was written to explore something else. Something rather less sexy. What if Britain never had its own revolution, but like so many European states after WWII, had become 'Communist' anyway thanks to Soviet bayonets?

The result is, at times, drab and dull. But at others, refreshingly different from reality. Still others, almost upsettingly sinister. It seems only right that the home of Orwell would lend itself so well to becoming a state that veered a little too closely to Airstrip One. My research into the Eastern Bloc (for which Dr Mark Smith, who lectured on the subject at Leeds, deserves thanks) led to a primitive understanding of the relationship between both citizens and government, and government and Moscow. I hope my take on how a Soviet Union with a far larger sphere of influence (it is the Antwerp, not Warsaw, Pact) rings somewhat true to Sovietologists far more experienced than myself.

I also apologise for the reasonable dose of 'handwavium' deployed here and there in the story. George Lansbury selling off the Royal Navy is – to my knowledge – a new way to make the notorious German Operation Sea Lion a success, but I freely accept it is itself a highly implausible event. I needed a way for the Red Army, not the US Army, to liberate Britain. I found one. What follows is the real work of the timeline – in Cripps, we see intellectual socialists compromised into Moscow apparatchiks. In Latham, we see a relatively unknown bureaucrat from our world become a long-serving dictator. A different Enoch Powell serves as our Dubček (inspired by a conversation he had with Margaret Thatcher in real life, where he stated he would fight for Britain under any government, including a communist one), and Vic Feather draws the short straw of representing stagnation. And so on, and so on. I hope these ideas – recognisable to Poles, Czechs, Russians and others, but alien to a land that has been (relatively) democratic for about a century.

As in almost all my timelines, there is also a fair amount of irony at work here. I hope these 'allohistorical coincidences', where they occurred, brought a smile to your face, or at least made sense. *Meet The New Boss* is perhaps my favourite thing that I have written alone, and I hope you enjoyed it.

Further thanks must go to the community at AlternateHistory.com, who read the original version and whose feedback was vital in getting it finished and up to scratch. Jack Tindale is responsible for the striking cover and the map in Appendix B, and I must thank Martin Dyer for making the final version of the Commonwealth of Great Britain's flag (based on some rough ideas of my own), which you can see in Appendix A. In addition, my fellow authors at Sea Lion Press have made the publication of its second wave of books – of which this is a part – much easier and speedier than it would otherwise have been. They have my utmost gratitude.

Tom Black
September 2015

About the author

Tom Black graduated in History from the University of Leeds in 2012. Having discovered alternate history as a teenager, he made his earliest attempts at it during his first year of university. After joining AlternateHistory.com, his hobby grew into a passion, and in 2015 he decided to start Sea Lion Press with fellow writers he had met through AH.com.

His other works, available through Sea Lion Press, include *For Want of a Paragraph*, in which David Miliband challenges Gordon Brown for the Labour leadership; *Zonen,* a tour of a world in which Denmark joined Britain and America in occupying part of Germany after the Second World War; *Boristopia*, a set of snapshots from a world where Boris Johnson's rise is radically altered; and (with Jack Tindale) *Shuffling The Deck*, a re-ordering of Britain's post-war Prime Ministers. He is also a contributor to Sea Lion Press' various collections of vignettes.

Tom also writes plays and other non-alternate history work. He co-wrote *Inheritance Blues* and *The Sunset Five*, two pieces by DugOut Theatre. He lives in Croydon, South London, and works for the *Croydon Citizen* news magazine.

Sea Lion Press

Sea Lion Press is the world's first publishing house dedicated to alternate history. To find out more, and to see our full catalogue, visit **sealionpress.co.uk.**

Sign up for our mailing list at **sealionpress.co.uk/contact** to be informed of all future releases. To support Sea Lion Press, visit **patreon.com/sealionpress**

Printed in Great Britain
by Amazon